A UNiCORN, a DINOSAUR, and a SHARK

Were Riding a Bicycle

For all the unicorns, dinosaurs, and sharks
who like to tell their own stories—JF

PENGUIN WORKSHOP
An imprint of Penguin Random House LLC, New York

First published in the United States of America by Penguin Workshop,
an imprint of Penguin Random House LLC, New York, 2024

Visit us online at penguinrandomhouse.com.

Library of Congress Cataloging-in-Publication Data is available.

Manufactured in China

ISBN 9780593519493   10 9 8 7 6 5 4 3 2 1 HH

A **UNICORN**, a **DINOSAUR**, and a **SHARK**
Were Riding a Bicycle

No, we weren't.

BY JONATHAN FENSKE

Penguin Workshop

A unicorn, a dinosaur, and a shark were riding a bicycle.

Fine.

A unicorn, a dinosaur, and a shark were TALKING about riding a bicycle.

Is that better?

And DREAMING about how much fun it would be to ride a bicycle.

Because you are in a book about unicorns, dinosaurs, and sharks!

You need to do unicorn, dinosaur, and shark things!

Oh. Like "ride a bicycle"?

Okay. Maybe that is not the best example.

But that is BORING.

Nobody wants to read a book about unicorns, dinosaurs, and sharks RELAXING!

Um. News flash: Somebody is reading one **RIGHT NOW.**

But in a **GOOD** book the characters do not do **BORING** things.

In a **GOOD** book the characters do **EXCITING** things.

Okay. I will do something exciting.

Will you ride a bicycle?

NO!

I will tell a story.

Hey! That's MY job!

Once upon a time, a delightful unicorn, an amazing dinosaur, and a magnificent shark were sitting quietly in a book.

The shark was FLOATING.

Yes, the shark was FLOATING.

What the unicorn, dinosaur, and shark wanted to do most in the world was relax and dream about rainbows and snacks.

LOVELY RAINBOW

YUMMY SNACK

I guess I, the impossibly cute T-shirt-wearing kitten narrator, will have to ride the bicycle.

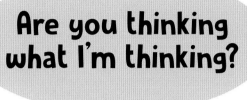